With love,
Anne Athena Dura

Iris Woke Up

Iris Woke Up

Anne Athena Dura

Iris Woke Up
illustrated edition

Copyright © 2023 by Anne Athena Dura
All rights reserved. Independently published
by Anne Athena Dura. This book or any portion
thereof (including illustrations) may not be reproduced
or used in any manner without the author's express
written permission except for brief quotations in a
book review.

anneathenadura@gmail.com
www.anneathenadura.com

ISBN: 978-1-981-05385-8

First published in 2018

Edited by Carlo DeCarlo
Cover Design Copyright © 2023 Anne Athena Dura
Illustrations Copyright © 2023 Anne Athena Dura

Dedicated to the one who's always been there,
from the day we met,
without any judgement,
without any reservations.

To the first person who read this story
and all of my stories.

To the person I know I can rely on
now and in the future.

To my partner in life,
my team, my mate,
my Vangelis.

Together we learn, we grow,
we make mistakes,
we discover ourselves,
we flourish and thrive.

To the one who accepted my flaws
and loved me enough
to agree to grow old with me.

Foreword

The idea for a story like Iris Woke Up was born on a bus. I pictured Percy, a child, as the protagonist, who kept waking up to the same nightmare over and over. I would have given his name a nice Greek equivalent; it would have been Perseus.
I played the story in my head, one scene at a time, and it didn't work out. How much do I really know about being a little boy in Greece? I gave up on the story and moved on to other projects, some published and some unreleased. The idea resurfaced unexpectedly in early 2018. It was the old story but a new one, too. Same, but different. This time, a teenage girl was in the picture, replacing Percy. At first, I had trouble finding a short, memorable name with a nice Greek equivalent to it. I cannot recall how I got 'Iris,' but it's the perfect name in retrospect. Besides, Percy kind of reminds me of the lightning thief.

In 2018, I began my penitent journey as a miserably fulfilled PhD student, studying Santorini's volcano (among other Greek ones), and that's when I decided to use the island in the story. I could have chosen an imaginary place, a town named Katsiki (meaning goat in Greek). Perhaps that would have been wiser. My similes and metaphors could have had deeper meanings, too, but I'm afraid I'm going to disappoint many readers who expect this from me. I'll be frank: It's just a story.

Some parts were inspired by things I've seen or heard throughout the years. Things that have no connection to each other somehow found a way to connect with the rest of the thoughts that roamed inside my head at random parts of the day when I should have been doing other things, like studying or sleeping. What is a story, if not just a series of thoughts put into order to create some place magical where we can all get lost for a day or two, for an hour or two?

With that said, maybe Iris Woke Up isn't just a story. Perhaps no story is just a story. It's a gateway. A getaway. It's an escape from whatever haunts us in our lives outside of the pages. The demons we have tucked in a drawer away from public judgment. The ghosts of past lives reminding us of who we could have been. The hollow feeling that stems from indulging in worthless schemes. But who is to say what is worthless and what isn't?

If you asked me, I'd say that Iris Woke Up is just a story, like all the other stories I've written in the past. But then again, to me, it is not just a story. Read on and draw your own conclusions.

The illustrations were also birthed from a random wandering inside the alleys of my mind. I had just finished reading Rupi Kaur's *the sun and her flowers* and thought to myself, I want to do something like this. No, not poetry. Illustrations. I want to give it a try and fail and try again and fail again. I took a drawing class about a million years ago but am no artist. Iris Woke Up, however, feels very personal to me (like all my writing endeavors anyway) to let another person into this world. Maybe I'm having trouble delegating. Nevertheless, I sat down on a Tuesday afternoon and sketched and sketched until I could sketch no more and decided to go for it. Is it just me, or are all enlightenments made on a Tuesday afternoon?

Dear reader, I hope you pardon my weak lines and expressionless faces. I tried my best to capture the emotions that have lingered ever since Iris visited my thoughts.

Dear reader, I hope you enjoy it.

Prologue

I sat on the most uncomfortable chair ever constructed.

"Who sells these things?" My thoughts wandered. "Who is in charge? Gosh, I stink. I have not gone home in a week. No one has. We are all worried."

I felt guilty. A little. I did not support her enough.

I stared at her pale face. She did not react. She did not care. I wish she would look at my soul.

"I brought you daisies," I would say.

"My favorite," she would respond.

"I know."

I knew she loved daisies. And I knew she loved flavored coffee.

Taking my eyes off her porcelain skin was impossible. Her face so peaceful. Her lips juicy. Her hair black as coal.

I preferred to be alone with her, but they would not let us. They barged in and out. No warning.

I held her hand. Should I tell her I love her? Would it make any difference?

My poor brain lay confused at the back of my head. Where do we go from here?

I turned to my right. The woman in white stood in the same spot. Motionless. Where was the other guy? He kept disappearing a lot. We needed him.

The walls surrounding us were as white as a ghost. Death watched every move we made. I was aware of his presence. Stronger than any other day. He understood no one could escape him.

I feared the time she would encounter him. Would she handle it? She was strong.

I paused my thoughts for a moment or two.

Was she?

Part 1

there's a piano in the kitchen
there's a piano in the kitchen

I

The smell of fresh daisies invaded her nostrils as she barely fluttered her eyelids. Iris did not open her eyes.

Her legs demanded to be repositioned. A soft yawn forced its way through her mouth. Iris wrested her back. Schools are closed on weekends. A smile painted itself on her face as she unfolded her arms. She let out a smooth sigh of contentment. Light penetrated the room through the clear curtains. Rose walls, fuchsia bed sheets, salmon drapery, and coral furniture.

Santa Claus's present lay with her: a porcelain doll. The back of her hand caressed the doll's silvery dress.

"Hello, Iris. We'll have a picnic today!" She sat up and held the lovely doll in front of her. "Dad says I can't bring toys with me." She smirked. "But you're not a toy." Her simper widened as she pulled her little friend near her chest. She placed her index finger on her mouth with a "Shh."

"Iris."

Iris jumped.

"Mom!" She arranged the doll on her pillow and dashed to the door. The six-year-old girl threw her arms around her beloved parent, who was so tall Iris ended up embracing her knees. Tall with long blonde hair and blue eyes.

"We will have our breakfast in nature today, remember dear?"

Iris nodded and rushed to her wardrobe to examine her pink clothes. At last, the summer pouffe dress that matched her honey eyes.

Iris's father started the engine. The girl jumped into the back seat and raised her arms instantly as they drove away. A basket carried their breakfast.

"Yoo-hoo!"

She beamed at the oval face in the rearview mirror. His thick dark hair danced with the wind. Iris tried to remember the day the hair on his temple turned gray; he was not that old.

Tall trees obstructed the view beyond. The family strode on the most greenish grass nature had ever devised. And above the emerald landscape floated the azure sky. Iris's mother often took her to this park after school.

Iris made herself comfortable on the grass. She chewed on a mouthful of a salmon sandwich. She closed her eyes and let out a soft note in delight.

"School ends soon," the father said with his usual thundering voice. "Have you contemplated spending the summer constructively?"

Iris cleared the black curls from her face gracefully with one hand. She chewed faster and swallowed before replying. "I have considered joining a music camp."

"What a splendid idea." A phony laugh accompanied the mother's applause.

Iris's parents nodded at one another with satisfied grins on their faces. The girl turned to study the surrounding animals that had scarcely caught her attention before that moment. Six black lambs eating grass. A thousand wagtails, she suspected, fluttered overhead. Whispering. Iris closed her eyes and listened from the distance.

"We should inform her."

"No."

"She has to know."

"She has to discover it by herself."

Iris opened her eyes in awe at the curious incident.

"Mom, listen!" She turned to her parents, who had been motionless for the last five minutes. "Mom?" She called, shaking, her heart beating faster. "Dad?"

They sat paralyzed.

Iris turned back to the lambs. To her surprise, the birds had vanished. The whispers had stopped. She stood up and crept towards the lambs. They appeared busy munching. It wasn't long before she realized the lambs were not devouring the grass, but rather the wagtails. Iris gasped at the sight of animal blood. That instant, her knees failed her. She stumbled.

"Aaaaaaaargh!"

Her right hand landed on the peak of a rock.

Iris's cry startled the lambs. The rock she fell on was razor-sharp, unlike the other rocks on the ground. She could not remember its existence a moment ago. It seemed to appear only to injure her. She cradled her wounded palm under her left elbow and puckered her face. The bitten wagtails before her flopped their wings and flew away. The lambs chased them into the woods.

Iris glared at the grass where the little birds used to be. The blood coating the shoots reminded her of cherry stains. She burst into tears.

"Maaah," she cried.

Her parents remained immobile. Something was different though. Their skin peeled. Decayed.

Sobs echoed across the land. Loneliness swamped her chest. Her head became warmer as her sobs grew louder. Iris fell on her knees. "Heeeeeelp m-me-he," she pleaded. The screaming echoed repeatedly.

Sudden silence.

Warm breathing stroked the back of her neck, raising the scant hair that grew there. Iris froze. She goggled in sheer dread, her mouth dry. A big furry animal crawled next to her. Its brown fur seemed golden in the daylight. Lingering on the left side of her body, five times her size, was a wolf.

Its tail swept across her face as it walked away from her. "Please, go away," she begged in a low voice.

2

Iris gasped for air as she flashed her eyes open. Another ordeal. Odd, graphic, and vivid. She settled her back for a minute or two, struggling to catch her breath. Sweat streamed from her warm forehead, her clothes soaking wet.

Inexplicable things appeared again in her dream. She wondered whether there was a way to realize she was in a dream before things got tangled. That way she could control it.

She evoked her childhood dreams.

Sometimes alongside Peter Pan, she flew across Europe. Other times, she ran from her zombie Grandma who spoke Hebrew. Bizarre dreams. Yet in none of them could she have been positive she was not awake.

She sat up and shoved the black curls away from her face. Those were not her parents, but the couple who lived downstairs — in that movie The Ones Below. She sighed. It was a story of a couple who sought to abduct the baby of their neighbors to make up for losing their own child.

Iris shivered at the thought of the horror movie.

Both her real parents had black hair and brown eyes. People assumed they were siblings. The most peculiar thing with couples. People pick partners whose beauty contests theirs, and as a result, they end up with partners who look like them. Iris faced the same issue in her relationship. At first, she thought people did not accept same-sex couples as a default reaction. To her surprise, however, it was because she was dating someone at the same level of attractiveness as her that people mistook them for sisters.

Opposites attract, but similarities bond.

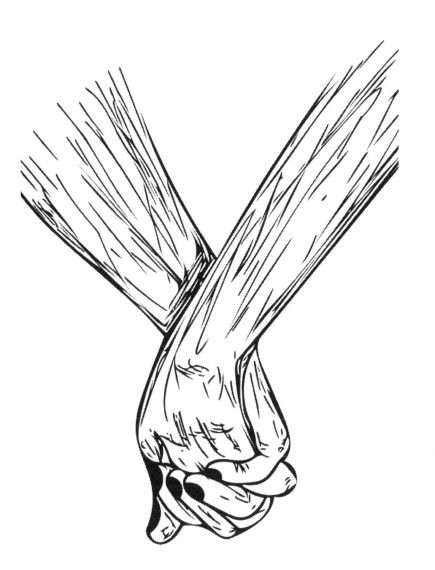

Her parents were both musicians. Violinists in the same orchestra, though they met in a different setting: a football game. Aaron went to see the game with his friends. His eyes fell on Samantha. Black hair, and skin so pale, so pure, it was nearly transparent. Her veins rose to the surface on the inside of her elbow. Aaron was a huge fan of smooth and flawless skin.

Samantha had attended the game with her soon-to-be-ex-boyfriend. She secretly sought to escape it. At the first opportunity, she headed straight towards the exit and into the jazz bar nearby.

Aaron left his friends to follow her into the bar. Back then, that kind of action was considered romantic. Today, men like that are creepy stalkers.

Iris stood.
A soft laughter.
She removed her wet clothes and used them to mop the sweat from her forehead. She struggled to the bathroom's cupboard. Towels, toilet paper, creams — there it was at the back of the cupboard: the thermometer.
Thirty-nine degrees Celsius.
Iris drew herself to the kitchen to brew coffee.

The coffee machine imitated the noise of a rat nibbling cardboard. What she loved most in her kitchen was the piano, right next to the fridge.
The ten-year anniversary gift from her girlfriend. Ten years of harassment, shame, and fear. Not the respect and endearment they deserved.
She sat on the piano stool, took a sip of her warm coffee, and placed it on the top.
Iris straightened her back.
What's happening?
Manipulated like a puppet, she could not control her muscles. What does a puppet feel? Her arms before her, arched fingers above the keys and a deep breath.

Anne Athena Dura

Do-Re-Mi-Fa-Sol-La-Si-Do

Do-Re-Mi-Fa-Sol-La-Si-Do

She played the same notes repeatedly using her left hand. Her right hand rested in midair.

Do – Mi – Sol

Her shoulders softened. Without free will, she nodded, a slight twinkle in her eyes. Then, her arms hung loose. She mastered her own limbs again.

As she stood, she took her cup from the wooden piano. A coffee ring visible where the cup used to be.

"Good job," she derided. "Never place warm cups of coffee on wood."

Without proper regard, she spilled her coffee over the piano.

"Not better." Her voice timid as she sensed something was not right.

She placed the cup on the sink.

Excruciating pain struck at the lowest part of her spinal cord.

"Aaaaargh," she cried.

Iris fell to her knees. She crawled out of the kitchen. The bitterness crept up her spine until she stifled a cry. She tried to get up but failed. Her head became heavier as the fever got worse.

Iris submitted to the insurmountable force. She lay exposed on the freezing floor, allowing her mind to be gradually subsumed in oblivion.

3

Iris gave in to the irresistible need to move her limbs. She pulled the bedsheets over her head and breathed. "Just breathe," she told herself.

She repositioned her body once or twice to make herself comfortable. Her hand ran through her forehead. Another dream.

Sunday, 10 February 2018, 6:45 a.m.

Iris tossed the phone on the other side of the bed. She was not gay, was she? At least her parents' description was accurate this time.

A dream within a dream. What now? Her head poked out of the sheets. Was she still dreaming?

Before her stood a wooden bookshelf right next to the window. Gray curtains blocked the sunlight. The whole bedroom was decorated in colors of white, black, and gray. No unnecessary embellishments. The way she remembered it. She untangled the sheets and brushed the warm carpet with her toes.

With one deep breath she examined the house. The piano was not in the kitchen. Her lungs overflowed with relief the moment she realized everything was in the right place.

Back to her bedroom, towards the bookshelf. She examined the books. The Invisible Man from Salem — she had never read that one. She reached for the book and took it in her hand to read the description.

"A Leo Junker story. Why not?" She bit her lower lip and crept back into bed. Making herself comfortable, she read the first chapter.

4

Iris stared at the translucent curtains. The sky seemed cloudless. Greece had a suitable weather for sun lovers like her. The reason Jacob had such a beautiful tan all year. She never got that tan while in Santorini. In Syros neither. Syros did not have great beaches, though. And its opera was small.

Twelve days until the Syros concert. She wanted Jacob to be there.

Iris's thoughts strayed as she got up. No strange dreams this time, thankfully.

She ambled to the kitchen and pressed the little button of the heavenly device that dripped the elixir of the gods. Such a convenience to prepare coffee before going to bed, then just push a button in the morning.

She stepped into the shower right after brushing her teeth. Iris let the freezing water straighten her hair. The water embraced her skin as she focused on her breathing.

"A live concert is approaching. Prepare. Cut out all distractions."

This concert was the only way she could prove to her parents she had made the right choice becoming a pianist instead of following their path.

Iris was an amazing violinist. Her love for the piano keys, however, was incomprehensible.

At twelve, her parents made her play for the Performing Arts School auditions. The auditions were separated into three sections: music, dancing, and acting. Her parents signed her up for the musical section without a second thought.

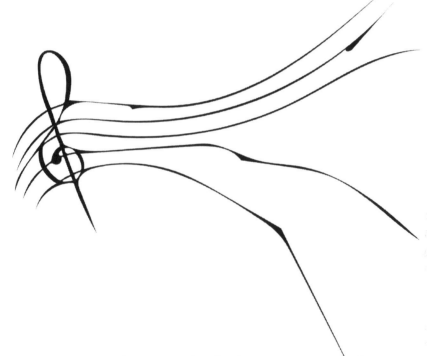

Iris secretly registered at the theatre section too, where she performed a monologue from Chekhov's The Seagull. It felt right.

They accepted her in both departments, which she most certainly did not predict. She kept it a secret from her parents though. They never found out. It was a topic not approachable for discussion.

Iris joined the orchestra shortly after that. An aspiring violinist. The media went mad about unravelling the secret life she withheld.

In school, she had to learn to play the piano plus one instrument of her choice. The flute.

Iris stepped out of the shower and wrapped a towel around her chest. The towel was so huge it covered her down to her knees. She then swaddled her hair in a smaller one.

Coffee was now ready. She could smell it as she strolled out of the bathroom. The familiar scent of a warm cup of happiness. Especially if you enjoy mixing different kinds of coffee blends with flavored syrups — vanilla, chestnut, cherry, caramel, strawberry, banana — plus the various types of milk: almond, hemp, coconut, rice. Anything you could imagine. Most people enjoy mixing flavors in cooking or baking. However, Iris enjoyed a cup of homemade, multi-flavored warm coffee. Always a warm one; never cold.

Iris prepared her coffee and glanced over her shoulder. The kitchen in her dream was like her kitchen in real life. Except for the piano, of course. A little round white table and two white metal chairs with soft pads stood where the piano was supposed to be. She walked towards the table and placed her coffee on it.

On the table next to the coffee was a white paper sheet covered in scribbled notes. Iris sat on a chair and held the paper close. She took a sip of her steaming beverage and reviewed her schedule for the day.

Iris Woke Up

8:00 Breakfast with Professor L

9:00 – 14:00 Orchestra rehearsal

14:00 – 19:00 Personal rehearsal

20:00 – 21:00 Gym

Iris put her daily schedule aside and savored her coffee. Then at home all evening for more piano. Until she was too tired. A typical day.

She set her coffee aside and walked to her bedroom to dress up. A blue linen shirt, a black skirt that shielded her knees, and a pair of comfortable shoes. Iris only owned comfortable shoes.

She looked at the black leather briefcase next to the door. She arranged her things the night before. Her books, phone, painkillers, tampons, gym clothes, towels, snacks, and a bottle of water; everything she needed throughout the day was in that suitcase-like bag.

Jacob would have laughed at her if he had seen how structured her life had become.

Jacob. A strong pain in her chest and a tingling sensation near her nostrils.

"Jacob," she whispered shaking.

She closed her eyes and took a deep breath, choking back her tears.

A glance at the rectangular clock above the sink forced her to gulp the rest of her coffee. Nineteen minutes to eight. Iris jumped up at once.

Grabbing her things, she rushed to her teal mini cooper. She placed her briefcase on the back seat and made herself comfortable right before putting on her seatbelt. Breakfast with her professor. Straight down the avenue. Then... where?

She had been there once. A cozy little café decorated as if it was from a different era. Everything in crème and brown. A huge park right outside. She sighed in despair trying to remember how to get there.

Twenty-first century. She took her phone out from an inside pocket of the bag and unlocked it quickly. Searching for google maps, something caught her eye. She went back to her home page, only to read the date and time.

Iris Woke Up

Iris froze.

Sunday, 10 February 2018, 7:49 a.m.

"Impossible." She rested her back. "It cannot be Sunday."

She glared at her phone. Was it stuck?

She got up and hurried to her house to check her digital calendar in the living room, leaving the car door wide open.

Something was not right. Another dream, Iris thought. She fell on her knees. When would this stop?
It has been a whole year of waking up in another dream or dreaming something illogical and spooky altogether. And the blackouts. All those times she could not remember how she got to one place.
Her therapist said she had been recuperating from her Post Traumatic Stress Disorder. The blackouts stopped a month earlier. But the dreams only got worse.
Iris lay on the couch. Was this real? Or was it her brain playing tricks on her again?
Iris sat up. She did not know what to do. Was she awake? She lost count of how many dreams she went through since the last time she was awake.
Iris glared at the wall opposite the couch. A portrait of her and Jacob hung on a rusty nail. The biggest portrait in Greece. She strolled towards the wall.
She ran her fingers over the picture of Jacob.
"Yiakobos," she tried to pronounce his name in Greek. "Yakovos," she tried again. "I never got your name right."
Cheeks heated as a tear sprouted from her eye.
Jacob would have known how to help her.

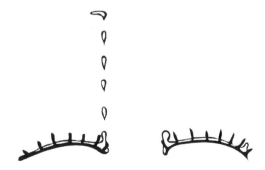

Iris Woke Up

She met Jacob on her trip to Greece three summers ago. Getting away from her toxic parents and all the fame that came with playing the violin. She had told no one. but deep inside, she hated the sound of the violin. Listening to it for as long as she could remember, she loathed it. When her parents bought her first violin, she was two years old. She craved to hurl it to the floor with all her baby might and smash every proof of its existence. So much rage in such a little child.

It was appallingly obvious to Iris after all those years. She remembered holding the violin and wishing to throw it outside the window. Two-year-old Iris just burst into tears instead.

How do you escape people obsessed with the violin when those people are your parents? You don't. You can't. At least not for many years to come.

In an attempt to get away from them at the age of fifteen, Iris transferred all the money she had earned from her brief music career to an account in the Greek National Bank. Then flew straight to Greece.

Visiting Santorini was a dream come true. Someone told her the pictures on the internet and the postcards were authentic. No Photoshop. Was it true? Was the sea as blue, and the landscape as alluring? The history of the island, the mystery of the volcano, the hospitable people, the sun. The wonderful tan she would get. It all fascinated her.

Iris Woke Up

Her money would have lasted at least ten years. She would finish school in Santorini. At first, she would skip school — for a year — to learn the language. Plenty of time ahead.

She had just arrived at her hotel, where she had planned to stay for a week before seeking a flat, but she searched for one right away. The sooner the better, plus she would spend less money that way. One hundred euros a night at the hotel, while most apartments were as cheap as four hundred per month. She had to act smart.

Her parents never believed she could do anything on her own. Yet there she was. On her own. She tried to fake a smile, but no feeling emerged from her chest.

Of all the apartments she visited, she immediately fell in love with one that had three rooms. She saw herself creating her own bedroom, a living room, a kitchen, and a bathroom. And there was one spare room where she would study.

As she looked at the empty space, the clean white walls, and the waxed wooden floor, it hit her. A piano filled the room before her eyes.

Yes, a piano.

Part 2

leave tonight or live and die this way
leave tonight or live and die this way

5

The smell of fresh daisies invaded her nostrils as she barely fluttered her eyelids. Iris did not open her eyes.

She tried to move her toes but failed. A deep inhale. A soft yawn from someone next to her. She flashed her eyes wide open. The room was bright. Light came through the window. Pink embraced her. Who was sleeping beside her? She failed to turn. Her limbs were paralyzed, as was her head. Only her eyes moved. They drifted. She recognized the room from her preceding dreams. Her heart hammered at that thought. A chill crept over her skin.

The person beside her moved.

A little girl with thick black curls sat up.

"Hello, Iris." The girl smiled. At once, Iris recognized the six-year-old from a previous dream.

Iris shivered. In a magical way, she had been transformed into a doll. A calm voice came through the crack. A knock on the door followed.

It was not magic, Iris thought. She was dreaming.

"Mom!" The girl fixed the doll on the pillow and rushed to her mother.

Iris waited for the child and the actress from The Ones Below to leave.

Her eyes rambled about the room. She struggled to move a finger or two, but nothing worked. The slightest movement was impossible.

Suddenly, something moved on the bed. The something crept towards her, her heart thumping faster.

From the corner of her eye, she distinguished the snout of a husky. Iris exhaled in relief. Without noticing it, she breathed heavily as she waited for the creature to enter her field of vision. Brown. It sniffed her. The animal's moustache tickled her toes. She tried to speak, but her facial muscles were unresponsive. The stuffed dog placed its paws on Iris and stroked her hard shell. The nails scraping against her produced a noise like scratching on a chalkboard.

Iris forced her eyes shut at once. The dense eyelids made a soft "ting." The dog's nose tickled her right arm. This time it no longer tried smelling her. It pressed against her body.

Iris opened her eyes at once. She battled to shake her head and yell "don't." Nothing happened. The toy pushed the doll to the corner of the bed.

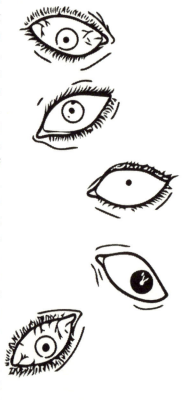

Iris's heart hammered. Her body temperature rose in fear. For a moment or two, she thought sweat dribbled down her forehead. Her porcelain fingers tangled among loose threads on the bedsheet, hanging at the edge.

"There's only one way out," said a voice inside her head.

Iris sank into nothingness. The distance between the top of the mattress and the wooden floor insinuated a never-ending fall. Gravity won. The porcelain body cut through the air. The silvery dress resisted.

Eyes wide open. Heartbeat echoed inside the room through invisible loudspeakers. She closed her eyes, focused on the sound of her heart. It was getting faster and louder, harder and heavier.

Her heavy frame hit the floor, causing the deafening sound that glass makes when smashed. Pieces of porcelain spread across the wood: big pieces, small pieces, and tiny ones.

The unseen speakers were silenced.

"One way."

6

The sun glowed over the metallic cars reflecting on Iris's pupil.
Delivery estimated five days, and day five was here. Excitement took over her untamed soul. The most delicate piano she had ever seen now belonged to her.
Just a week in her new apartment in Santorini. Already a double bed, a fridge, a stove, a laundry machine, and a piano. Still, only the necessary, she promised herself. No extra expenses.
Iris rushed to her white porch and sat on the front steps with a book in her hand. The book moderately engaged her. A tale about an emperor who commanded a wall be built around the city to isolate it from the world, saving the kingdom from the evil witch. Iris was not a fantasy fan. Why did she buy this book?
The witch turned into a young princess, seducing the emperor's firstborn. Her eyes rolled.

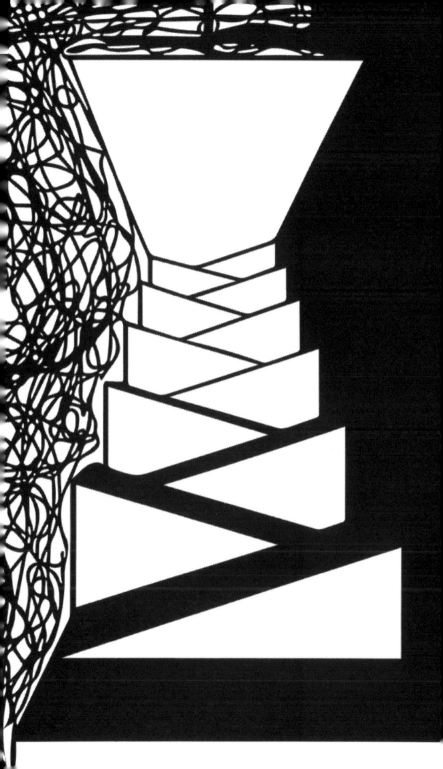

"I hope there's a good twist at the end of this story."

Iris jumped. Someone spoke. A boy stood behind her. Approximately her age. Dark hair and the tan she always craved. Had they met before?

"Yia sou," he said. She recognized the Greek word for "hello."

She smiled. The boy jabbered on with a large sentence she did not comprehend.

She looked for hints. Her feet bent closer. She moved to the right-most side, waiting for him to pass.

The boy moved forward and sat beside her. He said something in Greek again, pointing at the book. This time it sounded like a question. Iris exposed the cover. The boy nodded and spoke again. Iris glared at him for what seemed like forever.

"I don't speak Greek," she said finally.

"Oh, sorry," his accent heavy. "I'm Jacob. I live here."

The guy from whom she rented the apartment had a son named Jacob. They shook hands.

"I'm Iris."

"Are you here on vacation?"

"No, I'm here to stay." Iris wished the stranger would ask nothing else.

"Oh, permanently?" Jacob grinned.

"Yes." Iris stared at her feet.

"So, how come your parents moved here?"

"Um... I'm here on my own." Iris scratched her upper arm, letting Jacob know how uncomfortable she felt.

"Where are you from?" he asked.

"Ooooh." He jumped in excitement. "How do you say 'you're pretty' in Spanish?" "Canarias.

"Eres hermosa," Iris answered, then quickly added, "for a girl. Hermoso for a boy."

"Eres," Jacob tried, "ermoza."

Iris let out a weak giggle. "Kind of."

"Okay." Jacob nodded. "Will you go out with me?"

Iris translated that, too, but realized a moment too late he was asking her out on a date. She blushed. Before she could say anything, someone yelled across the street.

"It's here." Iris jumped up in excitement. "My piano!"

The man spotted her and did a gesture with his hand, leading an enormous van to the parking lot.

She led the men into her apartment. Jacob tried to help, too, but his skinny arms only allowed him to carry the stool.

Iris signed the papers and wished the men a good day before closing the door behind them.

"So, you play the piano!" Jacob fixed his eyes on the musical instrument.

Iris understood it might be odd to purchase a piano if she didn't play it. "I'm a musician," she explained. "I play the violin for a living. Though, I yearn to play the piano."

"Whoa! Really?"

Iris shrugged her shoulders.

"But you're so young."

Iris did not respond.

"Will you play for me?"

"No," Iris snapped. "My piano room is my personal space. I want you to leave."

"Ok." Jacob did not take it personally. "Will you let me buy you ice cream tomorrow?"

Iris smiled. "Sure."

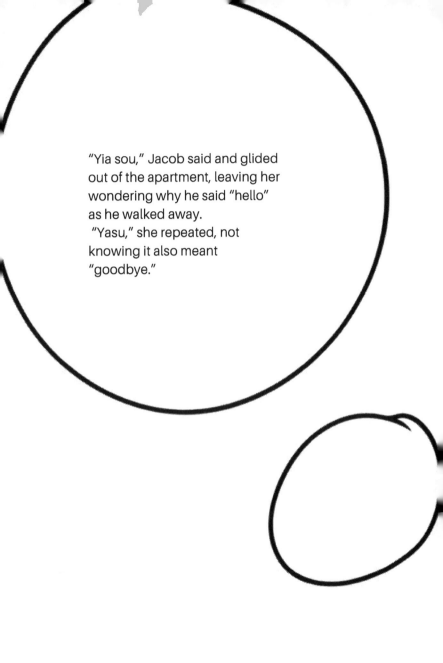

"Yia sou," Jacob said and glided out of the apartment, leaving her wondering why he said "hello" as he walked away.
 "Yasu," she repeated, not knowing it also meant "goodbye."

7

Iris sat motionless on the rusty bench. A row of ants formed around her feet. Each ant followed the one right before it. An endless line starting from their colony and across the park to the food they might bring home.
She leaned on the bench and sighed.
Thinking about Jacob was inevitable. His dark hair, his perfect tan.

Iris taught piano to children for two years before creating music again. Jacob found an invitation online to open auditions for musicians. Someone in Syros was filming a movie, and they needed conductors.

"This is huge," Jacob insisted.

"Yes," Iris agreed, "We've been through this. I won't choose a career over you."

"You won't have to." Iris faked a laughter as Jacob added, "I'm coming with you."

"Are you serious?" Iris flashed her most ecstatic smile.

"Come here." He wrapped his arms around her shoulders.

A surge of happiness flooded her chest. Moving to Greece was her best decision, she said to herself for probably the thousandth time in these last few years.

Her parents would think she was too young to live with someone — of course, she will live with him in Syros. At nineteen, she knew girls who were married, and some even had children of their own. No one had the right to judge how she lived her life. The couple had so many plans for their life together. They were perfect for each other.

Iris immediately bought tickets to Syros and packed her things. One week.

Little did she know she would miss the auditions. Little did she know their trip to Syros would lead to Jacob's inevitable death.

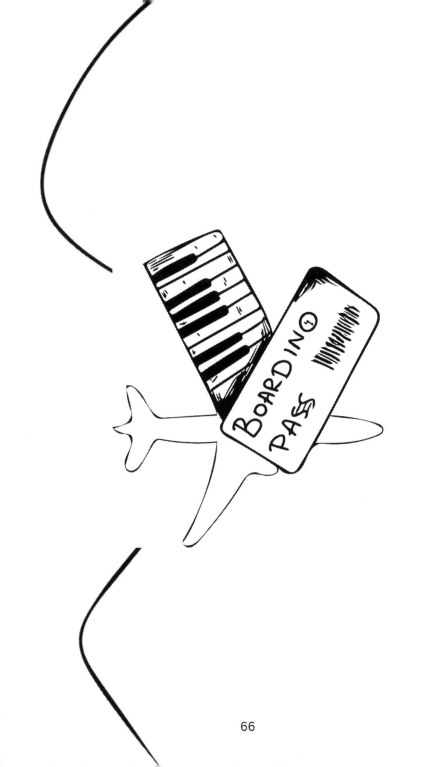

Iris stared at the ants' efforts to find food. She got up, careful enough not to step on any ants. Where should she go? Another Sunday.

The place reminded her of the lambs. The emerald grass, the wagtails, and the woods embracing it. Her eyes searched the land.

There it was. The wolf glared at her as if wanting to see through her. Paws stretched before it.

Iris shivered at the sudden thought that she could not remember how she got to the park. She gulped. At least this time she knew she was awake.

Between the trees unfurled an eternal, long road. She assumed she had to follow it home.

Without any notice, the grass withered. Gravel took its place. The landscape transformed before her eyes, spreading into infinity.

The woods perished, and the long road with it; but, the wolf remained. It rested. Motionless.

Iris looked around her once more, bewildered. This wolf has appeared in her dreams ever since she was little. It terrified her.

Yet she felt safe near it. The overwhelming sensation of the unknown filled her lungs. She had trouble breathing, as if it was water filling her lungs.

Iris coughed once or twice, then took a feeble step forward. The animal did not react, practically daring her to come closer. The altering landscape assured her she was not awake. The wild thing seemed ready for her to approach. Its eyes fixed on her figure.

She noticed a collar around its neck. She examined it closely. Leather strip, black, with a metal tag in the shape of a husky's head. Iris held the tag in her palm. Capital cursive letters carved into the metal.
"IRIS."
"Of course, your name is Iris." In no time, a warm surge of comfort and trust flooded her chest. She caressed the wolf's head. The creature made a mellow sound that reminded her of a satisfied dog, only this one was far scarier. She could not see its tail, but she was sure it was wagging.
Iris sat in between its paws. The animal remained still.

Anne Athena Dura

She relaxed her head on the soft brown fur. "What now, Iris?" she asked her new friend.

"Just wait."

Iris froze. The sound came from inside her head. Although her first thought was the wolf spoke in a voice of her own. "There's only one way out." The voice said.

Iris goggled. She tried to move away from the animal; instead, it blocked her. The wolf's left paw rested on both her feet, turning them numb.

"What is life, Iris?" the wolf asked in an exceptionally peaceful voice. "What is death?"

Iris swallowed. Those were not rhetorical questions. Then the voice added, "I need you to answer this for me. This is why I brought you here."

"Um," Iris thought about it for a moment or two. "Life is living, you know — when you breathe, your heart beats. And death is the opposite. When your heart stops beating, you stop being alive."

"What about when you're asleep? Are you alive then?"

"Yes." Iris was positive.

"Do not trust your eyes," the voice echoed inside her skull, "for they have betrayed you. And so has your memory. Don't let your dreams trick you into thinking you're awake."

"What's that supposed to mean?"

Iris Woke Up

"When you're dreaming, your brain creates images. Some are real, and others are not. When you see enough real images in a dream, you are tricked into thinking you are awake. But you're not, Iris. You haven't been in a long time."

"I know." Iris bit her lips. A tear slid from her cheek. Ever since Jacob died, she could hardly say what was real.

"Stop thinking about Jacob," the voice snapped.

Iris let out a soft sob. It was practically impossible, she realized. Jacob was a savior to her, something like a knight in shining armor who came into her life to change everything.

"When you believe you are awake in your own dreams, getting tricked into believing outrageous lies becomes smooth and painless."

"I don't understand," Iris cried.

"When did you see your parents for the last time?"

The last time she saw her parents — it was a late Friday night, at their dinner table. She got up with a "good night."

"You barely ate at all," her mother had said, worried.
"I'm not hungry," Iris had responded.
She had hurried to her bedroom, her parents' eyes following her. Closed the door behind her and went straight to bed. Relaxed her aching body on the soft bed sheets. The fever consistent. An excruciating pain at the back of her head — or was it her neck? She had not told her parents a thing so as not to concern them.

Iris's skin had been remarkably sensitive because of the fever; she could not bear the sensation of the bedsheets on her.

That was the last time she saw her parents before moving to Greece.

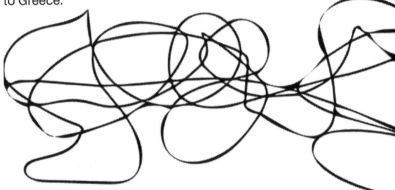

Greece," said the voice in her head. "Think twice."
The wolf lifted its paw from Iris's legs. The latter one tried to stand on both her feet as she got the message; she was free to go.

Without any warning, a strong pain exploded at the back of her head. She fell on her knees. The wolf hit her from behind.

"There's a way out," said the voice.
Iris raised her hand to the back of her head. She had barely touched her hair when a liquid poured across her fingers. She tried to keep her eyelids open but failed.
Iris fell flat on the gravel.

8

Iris gasped for air as her eyes flashed open. Fingers ran through her hair. Eyes darted about. Until finally...
A sigh. The relief of recognizing her bedroom.
"Only one way out."
Iris fled the house. She had to clear her thoughts. Her subconscious hinted a way to escape the horror every time she was dreaming. Was it the opposite of life?

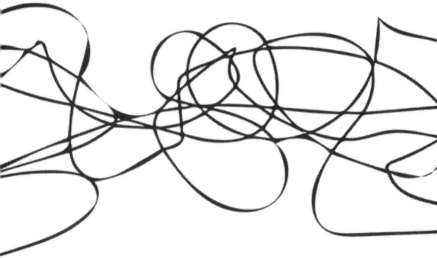

She headed straight into the only supermarket open on Sundays. Maybe cooking would help her get outside of her head. Oven-baked pastitsio. Pasta on the bottom, minced meat in the middle, and on top, some kind of milk-flour mixture she could not remember the name of.
The last time she tried, it was a failure. A hopeless attempt to impress Jacob by creating his favorite food.

She cracked her stiff neck. The pain followed her everywhere now. She ambled to the corridor with the pasta. She grabbed the plastic package and tossed it into the red basket. Number ten. Why is pasta numbered?

A step backwards. Someone stood to her right. She turned her head and recognized her neighbor at once.

"Chloe!"

Chloe turned to look at her. Stout with ash black hair and pale skin, faintly beautiful. She did not move. Her dark eyes squinted, and Iris raised her arm.

"Hey."

"Hi." Chloe seemed reserved.

"You okay?" Iris patted her on the shoulder.

Chloe took a couple of steps backwards. "Is this a joke?" Her voice shaking.

"It's me, Iris." A giggle.

"What?"

Iris raised her shoulders and laughed louder. "What's the matter with you?"

"What's the matter with you?" Chloe emphasized the last word. She shook her head and pointed at the glass-door fridges on the other side of the wall.

Iris followed her finger with her eyes. Her gaze narrowed as she dragged her feet to the refrigerators. Jacob's face stared back. She placed her index finger on her cheek.

Jacob did the same.

She looked down at her body. *She* was Jacob.

Anne Athena Dura

"This cannot be possible," she whispered. Iris lifted her eyes. Jacob's long face beamed back at her. "I must be dreaming," she realized. "I'm dreaming," she repeated, this time in a shrill voice. She turned to a puzzled Chloe and laughed. "Finally. I know I'm dreaming."

She embraced her neighbor. "I've almost solved it!"

Chloe pulled herself back at once. "What the —?"

Iris twirled. "How do I wake up now?"

Without any warning, a sharp demand to apologize pierced her chest. She faced Chloe whispering, "I'm so sorry," then stared at her, not knowing why she was sorry.

Chloe stood still with a bewildered look on her face. Everyone in the supermarket froze, Iris noticed.

"Mom,"
said
a
child,
"that
boy
doesn't
have
a
face."

She fixed her eyes on the glass before her. Jacob did not have a face, indeed.

Several steps later, she turned around and fled the market.

The doors automatically closed behind her. People at the market entrance gawked at her as she hurried by. She rushed to her car.

Within minutes she was driving in the narrow streets of Syros. How could she have missed this detail? Right foot pushed the accelerator.

"Wake up," she muttered to herself.

"Wake up."
Straight ahead, full speed.
Iris focused on Jacob's face. No other feature came to mind. None other than his tanned skin.

"Aaaaargh." Her scream reverberated inside the car. Foot pressed on the accelerator a little further.

Iris had been trapped in her dreams for a while. So long, in fact, she could no longer remember Jacob's face.

What was Jacob like? He doubtlessly had a marvelous tan. Iris tried to remember the very first day she met him. When she turned to the "Yia sou" he said.

Iris Woke Up

She sat on the front porch steps of the building, expecting her delivery. The young boy stood right behind her. He greeted her, then said something she did not recognize.

A warm August morning, sometime between nine o'clock and eleven, according to her shipping email. The sun was burning her pale skin. It shone over the front metallic part of a red Volvo on the opposite side of the road, causing a spark to fall into Iris's eyes. It forced her to wear sunglasses as she scrutinized a fantasy book.

She could hear the waves from where she was sitting. Blue waves were stroking the magma rocks on the coast, forming a white froth. Every single detail of that day was vividly etched in her mind.

She had met Jacob three summers back. The hair at the back of her neck rose at the thought that she had only been dreaming about meeting Jacob.

Focus! Jacob's face, the moment he introduced himself — it was plain. There was no face. Ever.

Iris tensely opened her window. The road lay flat and straight. She drove alone on a highway. The sky dark. The wind swirled through the window messing with her black curls. Without any warning, she burst into tears.

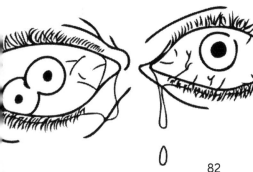

Iris pushed the accelerator harder. The front lights of her car, the only lights on the road. A right turn that exited the highway and entered a town she had never visited.
"WAKE U-HUP," she yelled, but she could hardly hear herself over the whoosh of the wind. She hit the steering wheel with her left fist. "Wake up!"
A wall appeared at the end of the road. She instinctively prepared for a left turn but changed her mind. Maybe this was her only way out.
Death. The opposite of life.
Iris turned on the radio as loud as her eardrums could bare.

"I had a feeling I could be someone..."

Wheel in her fists, arms fiercely stretched before her. She discerned the salt in her tears as they rivered from her eyes, her right foot rigid on the accelerator.

"Be someone, be someone..."

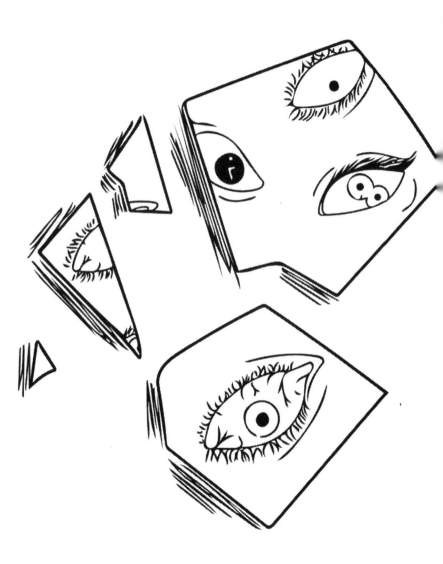

Iris crashed her car onto the wall at maximum speed. In a split second, glass shattered. The metal was deforming before her eyes as if it was made of rubber. At that point it hit her. She never left home. She never moved to Santorini. Pain instantly spread under her skin as thousands of shards of glass pierced her body just before her temple hit the steering wheel.

"You got a fast car, but is it fast enough so you can fly away..."

Iris stopped breathing. Her empty eyes fixed on the lake of blood around the car. It seemed black under the moonlight. Smoke came from the car. The scent of burning flesh.

"You gotta make a decision, leave tonight or live and die this way."

Part 3

the smell of fresh daisies
the smell of fresh daisies

9

I remember thinking it was unbelievable how weekends go to waste. Five full days before a break from school and the singing — yeah, singing is my passion, but I'm fifteen for God's sake. Just wanted to spend time with my girlfriend. Simple as that. Instead, I slept through most of Saturday, then I stayed up late only to wake up late on Sunday.

I remember thinking about how life was cruel.

When my phone rang, I almost choked on my peanut butter. Irida's mother was calling me. Only a couple of days ago, Irida said she finally came out to her parents.

Walking home on Friday, she gripped my hand. I whispered, "I'm not sure it's safe."

"Twenty-first century." Irida smiled.

I came out at eight. My family found it adorable. I knew I was gay, despite no sex drive yet. They laughed. They had it in mind, though, as I grew older. It was therefore easy for me to tell them at age fifteen that I had a girlfriend.

It was different for Irida, though. She could not determine if her parents were open-minded enough to accept her. Or was it simply her fear restraining her from being open?

I looked around and spotted a bench. I pulled Irida towards it. She explained how she talked to her parents about us earlier that day. A faint smile painted itself on my face. Her parents accepted it, she said.

For a moment or two, I wondered whether her mother was calling me about our secret relationship.

I held my black Samsung in my palm and hastily swallowed. I had to use my pinky to touch the screen and answer as the rest of my fingers were covered in peanut butter.

"Hello?" My heartbeat faster.

"Hi... um..." Irida's mother sounded inexplicably sorrowful, her voice low. She was choking back sobs, I realized.

A sharp pain penetrated my chest as terrible possibilities stormed inside my head. "Yes?"

I was not good enough for her daughter, right? Perhaps she learned my dad spent two months in prison at twenty-seven. Or maybe she found out about that one time I tried to smoke pot at a party two years ago. My entire life flashed before my eyes as I wondered why she was calling me.

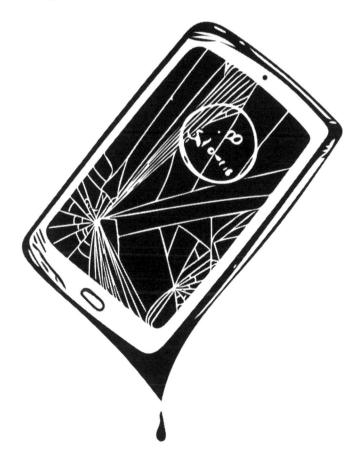

"I hope you don't mind my call. You should know—" She inhaled deeply over the phone.

My thoughts drifted. "Um... is everything okay?" My heart hammered. Something happened to Irida, and all I was worried about was what I might have or might not have smoked when I was thirteen.

"She... um..." Samantha hesitated. I sat paralyzed in my kitchen dreading what had happened. My arms numb. My jaw hung open, ready to scream something right after she spoke. I had nothing to say though. I waited. In my mind, the silence between us lasted five minutes, but it was probably a fleeting moment. "Well," Samantha finally spoke, "she could not wake up, so we took her to the hospital right away. She, ah... she's been sleeping for over thirty hours. The doctors say she might not be waking up soon."

I froze. Irida was dead. That was my first guess. I swallowed. I presumed she would have mentioned it if her daughter was no longer alive. The kitchen spun around me. My upper body tilted forward of its own will.

Samantha said something I did not hear.

"Wha-what?" My voice weak.

"She's in a coma," she said.

Her voice echoed. The phone slipped through and out of my grasp. I leaned on the back of my chair and stared at my plate.

Irida was in a coma.

10

My parents visited Santorini on their honeymoon. They loved the island so much, they stayed there.

I never expected Irida to be so enthusiastic when I told her I was born in Santorini. I never understood why she craved to visit the island.

Volcanoes fascinated her. I never saw a volcano though.

What did I see there? A caldera with a huge cliff, ugly white houses, and a bunch of noisy tourists minding everybody's business.

My parents did not like the health services though. They were concerned something might happen, and they would have to go to a hospital somewhere else, perhaps Athens. That led them to move to the capital of Greece two years ago.

I would throw tantrums for over a month because they never asked me. To my surprise, a thirteen-year-old's opinion did not matter to adults. The island was a terrible place to settle, but my friends lived there, everyone I knew.

I met Irida in Athens though. I remember secretly wishing she was gay the moment I laid my eyes upon her. Everyone called her Iris, but I preferred the Greek "Irida." Ancient Greek names are amazing. It is unfathomable why anyone would change it to make it sound foreign. I respect my parents for giving me a Greek name. The Spanish alternative they came up with was the classic "Camila." I am grateful they did not choose that. I could not imagine the harassment I would have been through if my name meant "camel" in Greek. Children are unforgiving of lousy names. The name Irida, I found, had various origins, which was captivating. The reason I admired the name so much.

I caught Irida staring at me with those gorgeous honey eyes regularly. My delirium was unbearable. That face was mesmerizing. She was nowhere, and then she was everywhere. On the bus, on the road, on television. I stalked her on Facebook. I flipped out. The agony had to end.

In the middle of the schoolyard. I approached her. A brave act. Being a non-Greek was not enough. I had to be discreet. All those hawks. Most kids at school were not homophobic, but a few opposed our — lifestyle.

My dad spent two months in prison for beating up a dude because he insulted my kind. My father is a wonderful person.

II

I have always hated hospitals. Everything is so white. Narrow corridors. Lights create The Walking Dead vibe. That smell — oh, the odor of death following you. You wash your hands only to sniff the lavender soap, but you can still smell it the instant the soap evaporates. It never leaves. Sometimes it gets into your home and lingers for a week. Like the unwanted guest who declared your couch for a couple of nights and ends up knowing which cupboard holds the jars with the spices several weeks later.

Irida lied senseless on the filthy hospital bed. I seized her hand. "You'll be okay," I whispered, wiping a tear off my cheek.

"She's lucky to have you." Samantha faked a smile.

I was well aware Irida secretly wished she preferred boys. A terrible revelation. I said nothing though. My affection was beyond vigorous desires and clandestine miseries. I sensed the trouble in accepting she was different. The media probed into her personal life. She had a reputation to protect; she could not risk standing in the spotlight due to her orientation. It would have been simpler if she liked boys.

I choked back my tears as I examined her pale face.

"Meningitis," Aaron said.

That would explain the persistent headache and fever. I swallowed. How could symptoms so common be indications for such a major health problem? In what world was that fair? I pondered whether Irida had been keeping other symptoms a secret. What if she missed the opportunity to be cured because she refused to communicate?

I shook my head. A teardrop warmed my cheekbone as I pecked her on the forehead, our hands still intertwined.

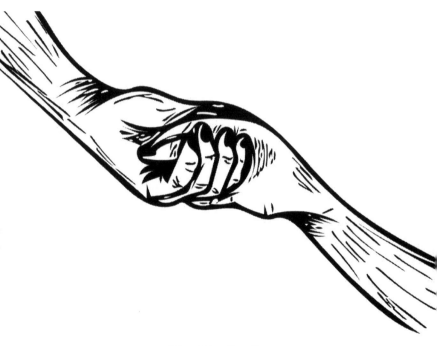

"You'll be fine."

I settled on the uncomfortable seat. It was my second day at the hospital. When Samantha called me, I threw on a dress and headed straight to the hospital. I had not left yet. Not once. The chair was itchy on my bare legs. I wished I had brought a spare pair of underwear. My head bowed to the left and touched my shoulder with my chin. I sniffed the air to ensure I did not require deodorant.

"Go home. Get some rest."

I jumped at the sound of Samantha's voice. She saw me. My cheeks blushed instantly.

"I'm okay." My eyes wandered. I wanted to stay. Even though I despised hospitals. My eyes were fixed on Irida's ailing face. Her parents left us alone.

I puckered my face. Irida's eyelids moved. I stared at her face, but nothing happened. Perhaps her eyeballs slightly moved; maybe she was dreaming. I wondered if people in a coma dream. Probably not. I suppose I was so drained that I saw things that weren't there.

Without any warning, the door swung open. Can't I ever be alone with her? A tall man stood by the doorway. I guessed he was Irida's doctor. Samantha mentioned his name — what was it —

"Dr. Iakovos Pappas," he said, then urged me to leave. I obeyed.

12

I arrived first at the Mall, but I did not mind waiting. Did Irida change her mind? I did not ask her out. I announced I would have frozen yogurt on Friday at 8 p.m. She asked to join me.

We knew each other from school. All our conversations revolved around how difficult homework was and how short the weekends seemed. It was easy to see she had trouble balancing her life.

When I mentioned I was born in Santorini, she said she wanted to live in Santorini one day. And when I explained I would choose Syros, she claimed she wanted to live in Syros. I stared at her. What should I respond?

I do not go to the mall. It is a camouflaged prison. Kids my age go there weekly and spend a full day wandering from stores to fast-food chains to the movies and back to the stores. It keeps you busy, the mall. You spend hours doing everything and, at the same time, nothing.

Outside the mall were enormous metallic sculptures of the letters T-H-E M-A-L-L. I had never seen those before. I sat on the letter T. Irida would show up any minute now. My eyes strayed. How convenient to build a massive mall right outside the train station.

Accessible is the keyword. A two-minute walk from the platform. Unless you were with friends, chattering and bantering. In that case, it took eons to cross the same distance.

I saw Irida's black curls from the corner of my eye. I got up at once.

"Hi." She smiled and threw her arms around my neck for a brief greeting ritual.

I hugged her back. "How are you?" A wisp of hair fell across my eyes as we pulled ourselves back. I removed the hair from my face and attempted a smile.

"Great! Frozen yogurt," she said. Her eyes twinkled.

"Yep." I jumped, and we walked towards the entrance.

"Where are you from exactly?" Irida asked me as we sat with our frozen yogurt.

"Canarias," I replied, then quickly added, "Well, partially. My mother is from the islands, but my father is half Greek and half Spanish — from Huelva." I ate my frozen yogurt. "He had never been to Greece prior to meeting my mother. Thank God I don't have a Spanish name. Could you imagine that?" I shook my head. "I like my name. Chloe. It's— it's so Greek. Young green shoot! What's more charming than that—?"

I stopped abruptly. I realized I was talking hastily and blushed. Irida was glaring at me with her striking honey brown eyes. I was sitting with a famous person at the mall, and all I was talking about was how much I loved my name. I looked at my spoon.

Irida was full Greek. Three months later, I found out she wanted to believe she was not.

I never knew what was in her head.

Irida also had a knack with languages, so I taught her Spanish — at home we only spoke Spanish with my parents. In about four months, she managed to hold a complete conversation. I only noticed when I caught her giving directions to a tourist in perfect Spanish.

We had a wonderful time together. We started as best friends until she was ready to reveal her biggest secret.

The night she told me she might like girls, I couldn't contain myself. I jumped up and kissed her full on the mouth. My arms hung awkwardly as I did not know what to do with them.

13

The corridor unraveled before me in the most mind-numbing way. When would this distress end?

I leaned on the vending machine to drink my cola. Before me on the corridor stood Samantha. I faked a smile and took a sip from my drink.

Samantha cleared her throat. "We cancelled the concert," she said. "Iris didn't want to be a part of it anyway."

"Wha—" I swallowed. "What do you mean?" My mouth dried up. I forgot about the forthcoming concert.

"When Iris was two," Samantha explained, "we gave her a violin. We expected her to like it. Instead, she burst into tears. Soon we found out she hated the violin. So, we offered her the chance to go to art school and explore her talents. Next thing we know, she failed the theatre auditions but kept it a secret. She never told us she registered for both music and acting." The woman sighed. A surge of pain rippled across her facial muscles. "Last week, we discovered she is interested in the piano. So, on Friday, Aaron and I announced at dinner we were planning to buy one for her. She did not respond. She got up and went to bed."

Irida never told me how much she hated the violin, but it was obvious. Her parents acknowledged she was playing it only for them even though they never asked her to. In a sick way, in her mind, she existed to satisfy others. Tell them what they want to hear.

Her favorite movie was my favorite movie, I recalled.

Her favorite food was my favorite food.

Her favorite color was green. And so was mine.

Was she trying to please me? Entice me? Possibly. It did not bother me. We spent our time with movies, music, and long walks. We played board games. And sometimes I would let her play my piano as I sang. Irida believed in my vocal capabilities. She always said I'd be the next Bonnie Tyler, though I wanted to be the next Janis Joplin.

I realized how little I knew about Irida. "She had a terrible headache," I said. "Was that the day, um—?"

"Yes, she came out earlier that day. It was fine — amazing, more like it. My point is," Samantha sat on a vacant seat, "she never talked to us. Not even about her headaches. She's so secretive about everything. And the only reason she told us about you — was for you." Samantha sighed.

I looked at my feet. Irida was enigmatic, indeed. She would never express her true emotions. Her reaction to everything involved tears. The only way she controlled a situation.

My dark eyes examined Samantha. Her hair had not been washed in a week. The skin around her eyes was bluish and swollen. Her lips pale. For a moment or two, her breathing echoed as she cradled her head in her palms.

I gulped the rest of my cola and threw the can into the bin. I trotted across the corridor and headed to Irida's room. Dr Pappas walked by me, avoiding eye contact. I stopped to follow him with my eyes.

He approached Samantha. She got up quickly and yelled, "Aaron?"
Aaron's head appeared behind the wall. He rushed beside his wife.
The doctor spoke again. Samantha grasped Aaron's hand as tears flooded her face.
My heart beat faster. Without any notice, I burst into tears. Aaron's face was so red, I thought it would explode. He puckered his forehead and turned to his wife, cushioning her head in his chest. Only then did I realize how short Samantha was.
I wiped my face with my sleeve and marched to Irida's room again. This was not happening, I convinced myself. Before I reached her doorway, a man blocked my entrance. I tried to force him aside, but he was heavier. He said something I did not hear.
I peered over his shoulder. Irida's lifeless body lay at the center of the room. A smile curved on her lips. A calm expression took over her facial features as if something horrible was now gone. Tears fell effortlessly from my eyes. I might have said something inappropriate to the man standing before me right before I kicked him on the knee, but I do not quite remember. He doubled over in pain. The next thing I remember, security dragged me out of the building.

2 years later...

Cemeteries appear amicable in the daylight. Sometimes I ponder about the first person who buried the dead. A religious act turned into a tradition. Or is it the other way around? Who initiated it? My father considered it as honoring the deceased. Bullshit. It's not like they know someone has buried them. The tragedy is for the living. They create fancy tombs to generate one more reason to keep their beloved ones with them, to cleave to their memories.

I cannot help but cling to Irida.

The pain in my chest is unbearable. The horrendous notion that I will never see her again warps my critical thinking. Her honey brown eyes pierce my brain each and every sleepless night.

Moving on is impossible.

I do not love her. I never did. We had fun times together, but "Love" at fifteen is a complicated perception. Yes, I was passionate. I empathized with her. And occasionally felt sorry for her.

Ever since she passed, I've been visiting her at least once a week. I bring nuts to feed the squirrels. I leave fresh daisies, and I inspect the enduring letters carved in the marble.

"Irida Iakoumatou," I read, "2003-2018."

I would hate myself if I forgot. Like her parents. It was easy for them. Their baby boy is turning one next month.

Wrestling with her absence is a nightmare. The smell of her skin lingers on my memory. Nightmares keep me awake at night. The sleepless nights make me sleep during the day. I had odd dreams about Irida being in Santorini with a faceless man. They still haunt me.

When I returned to school, I experienced the loneliest days of my life. No one would come near me. People imagined I carried a virus that would make them sick.

There should have been a carving on the gravestone saying, "Life is brief when you don't comprehend living."

That comes to mind when I reflect on Irida nowadays. She did not realize she never appreciated her life. She assumed she was not enough to satisfy people around her. As a result, she did not live.

I trusted the universe. I expected people in life got what they deserved at some point. Whether early in life or later. Life works in mysterious ways. We are all born for a cause, and Irida kept conflicting with her purpose.

I try to create a happy image of her.

My eyes roam over the cemetery. Cypresses intrude the peaceful scenery every here and there. Sunlight shimmers between their leaves. A squirrel chews the nuts I tossed on the ground. Another squirrel rushes to them, stuffing a couple into its mouth and climbing up the nearest tree to nibble them undisturbed. I did not imagine squirrels move that fast.

I look at Irida's picture. She smiles back at me. I am not sure about the afterlife. Does it exist? Does it not?

Back in elementary school, a teacher once told us "Koimeterion" is the original Greek word for cemetery. It originates from the verb, which means "to sleep." In the old days, people suspected we do not die, we only fall asleep — forever.

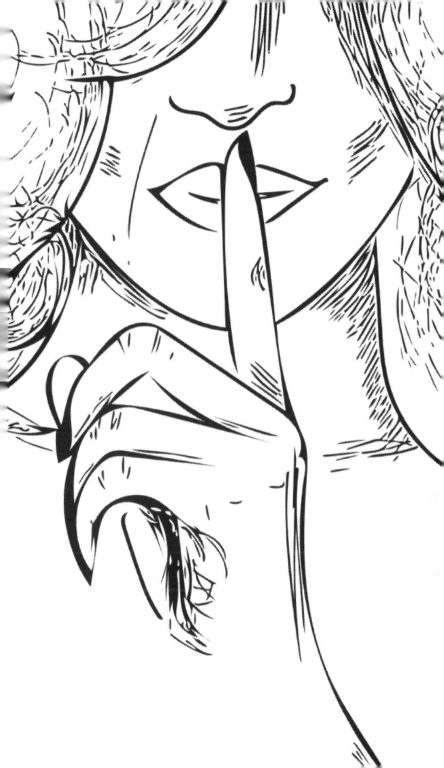

Perhaps, that is the afterlife. Perhaps, Irida is only sleeping till the end of time underneath my feet. I don't know how to feel about it. Nevertheless, it gives me hope to visualize Irida in a pleasant place in her dreams, living a life she deserved throughout eternity.

Anne Athena Dura

The
smell
of
fresh
daisies
invaded
her
nostrils
as
she
barely
fluttered
her
eyelids.
Iris
did
not
open
her
eyes.

Acknowledgements

A published book results from collaboration and help from many people, professionals or not. I may have written and illustrated Iris Woke Up, but others are behind it, too. The first person I would like to thank for their contribution is none other than Carlo DeCarlo, the editor of the second edition. With his experience and professionality, the book was ready for publication in no time. A special thanks to Stavros Birmpilopoulos, who edited the first edition of Iris Woke Up and made me believe it was a good story despite my insecurities.

But of course, this book would have never made it to the hands of an editor were it not for my oh-so-patient beta readers: Violeta Meli, Ilias Stasinopoulos, Katerina Nafsika Katsetsiadou, Christos Andrikopoulos, Chryssa Andrianopoulou. Beta readers are the lucky ones, though, the first to read an unpublished yet not-so-shitty manuscript. My sister, Christina, got to read a semi-descent version of it and gave me positive feedback, which meant a lot because she's always one of my most critical readers. She never shies away from telling me that what I wrote needs improvement, and I thank her for that; she's making me a better writer. I also thank the person who read the horrific first draft of the story and didn't run away, Vangelis.

This goes without saying, but I also thank my parents, who (my entire life) have treated my writing as plainly a hobby I would grow out of and yet have been very supportive in the last few years since I decided to publish my first story. A very special thanks to my mom who, in spite of not speaking English, sat down night after night with my debut novel, The Shadows We Live In, in one hand and a dictionary in the other and translated my work, word by word, little by little so that she could read my book, and I am sure she will do the same with the next ones, too. She never told me this; I found her notes one Tuesday afternoon, and it brings tears to my eyes whenever I recall it.

The next two people I want to thank didn't contribute to the book itself but were there from the first edition till now. They are Prof. P. Nomikou and Prof. T.J. Mertzimekis. They followed me through my journey as a PhD and saw me grow as a scientist. They supported me, pushed me to improve and respected me, giving me space when needed. My PhD began with the book's first edition, and now it ends with the release of the second edition. There is no better way to end this journey than combining the two things I love the most: fiction and earth sciences. I hope one day I make them proud.

Finally, I would like to thank Christos Azariadis, who has helped me as a friend, fellow writer, and amazing lawyer ever since I've known him. He lent a helping hand when I needed it without a second thought, and because of him, this book exists.

I also thank you, dear reader, for purchasing this book and supporting my dream. I hope we meet again.

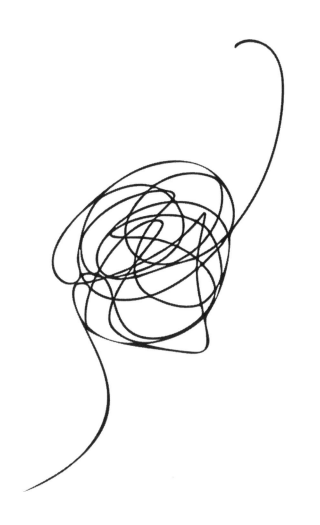

About the author

Anne Athena Dura was born in Tepelene, Albania, and raised in Athens, Greece by the most amazing people on this planet. She fell in love with the English language as a child and started writing short stories at a very young age. She has written and published several stories and hopes to continue writing until she could write no more.

visit
www.anneathenadura.com

Made in the USA
Middletown, DE
06 January 2024